The Coloring Book of
Fantasy Delights

By Randall L. Scott
Illustrations by Eric Hammond

The Coloring Book of Fantasy Delights
by Randall L. Scott
Copyright © 2018
ISBN: 978-1-944592-22-6
Cover and Illustrations by
Eric Hammond
All Rights Reserved

Volumes in the
Dark Tales Series

Available now on e-book:
Dark Dreams; an illustrated novel
Dark Journey; a short story
Dark Temple; a short story
Dark Realms; an illustrated novel
Dark & Deadly; a short story
Dark & Stormy; a short story
Dark Tomb; a short story
Dark Path; a short story
Dark Metal; a short story
Dark Descent; a short story
Dark & Deep; a short story
Dark Tales; a compilation

Now in paperback:
Dark Dreams; an illustrated novel
Dark Realms; an illustrated novel
Dark Tales; a compilation

By Eric Hammond:
A Coloring Book of Fantasy Journeys

Fantasy Lexicon -- an illustrated reference book
with over 1,200 uncommon words including
Thieves' Cant, fantasy words, jargon and
slang from the past
detailed and defined.

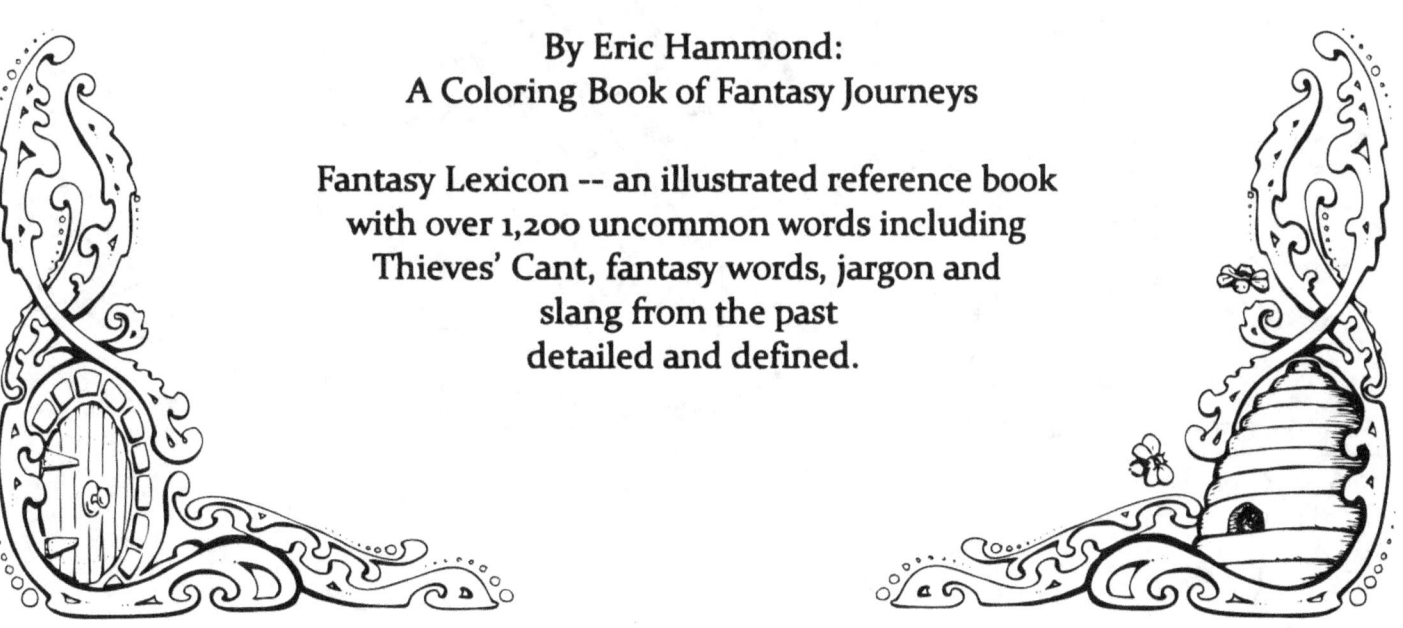

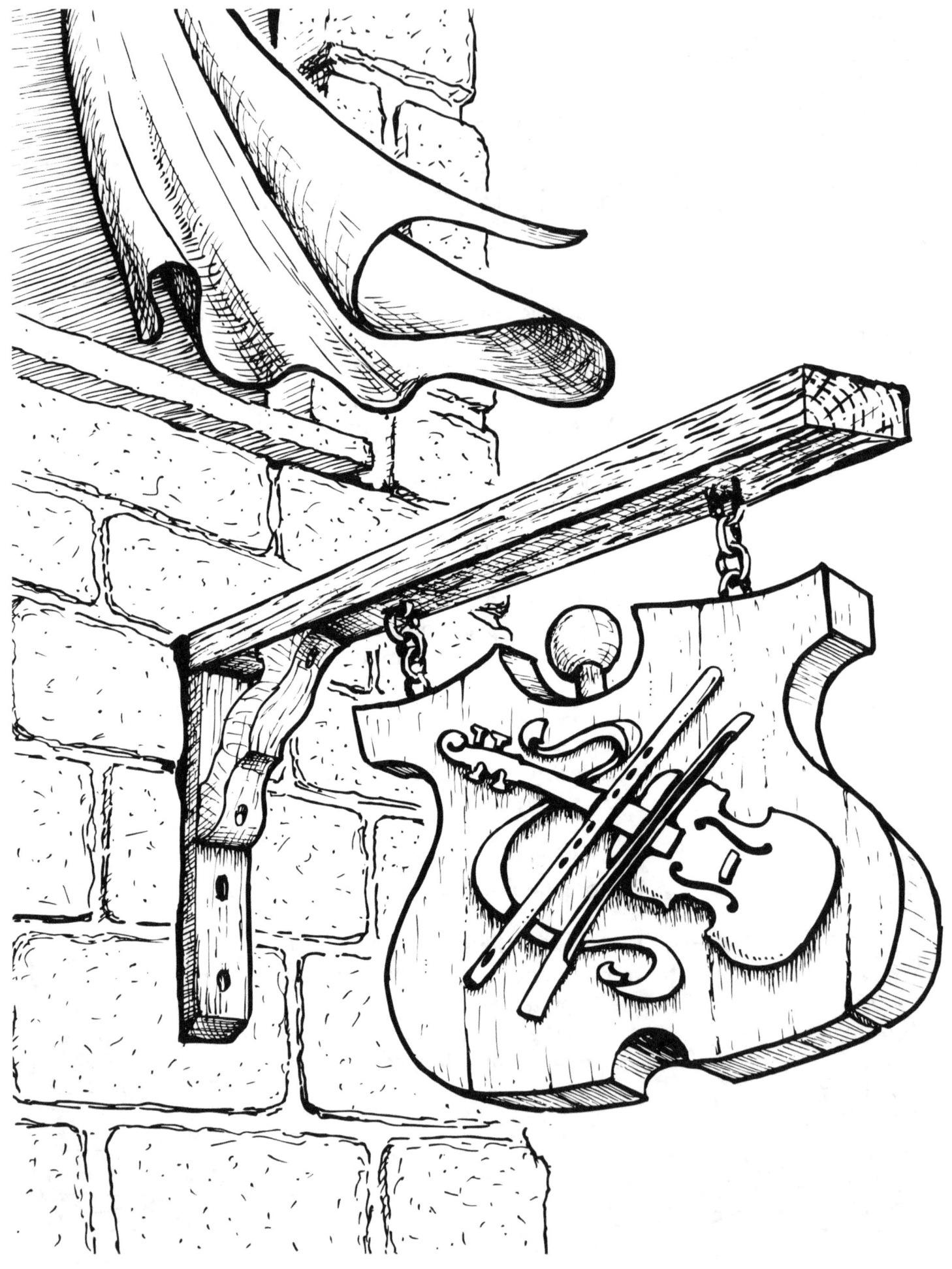

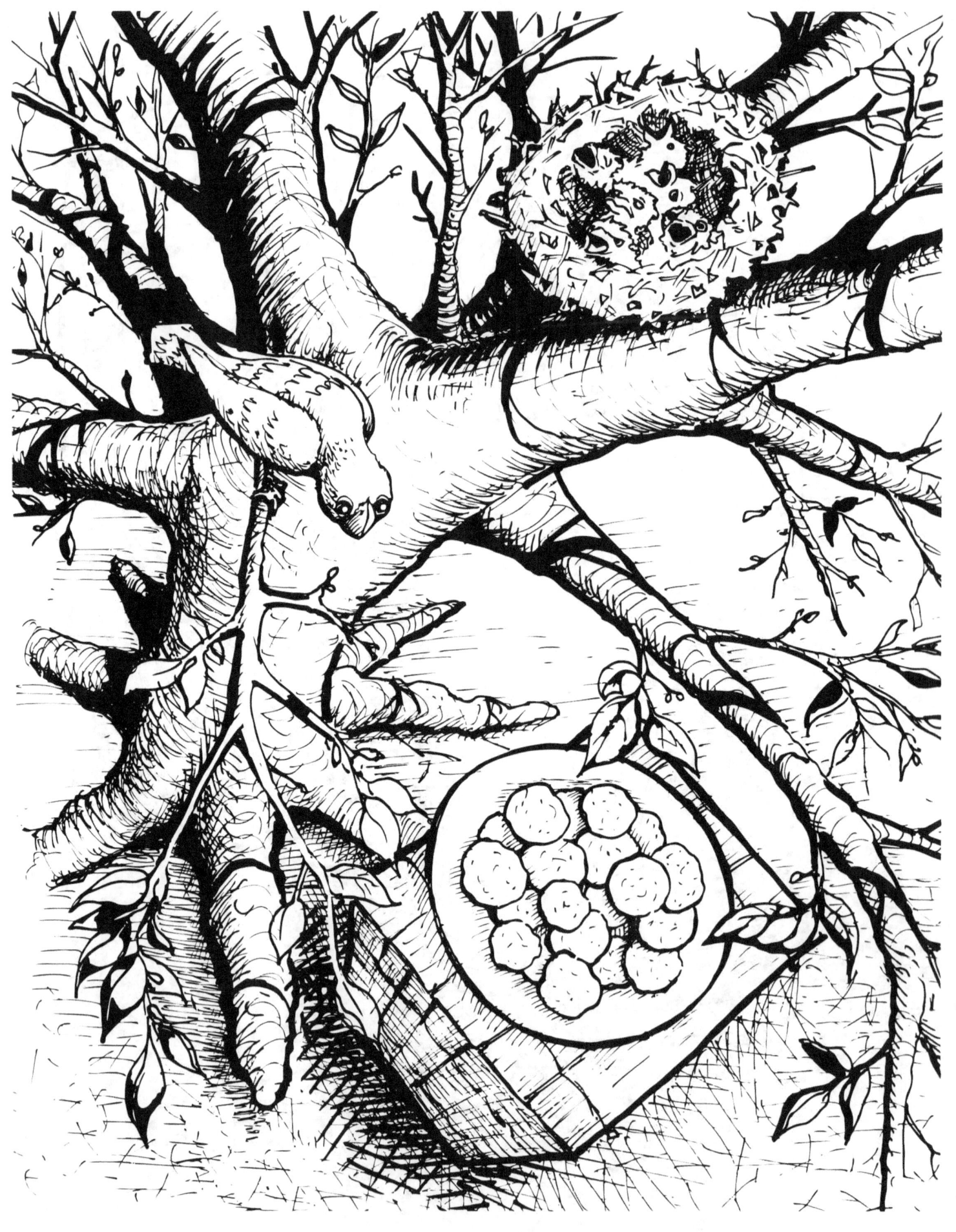

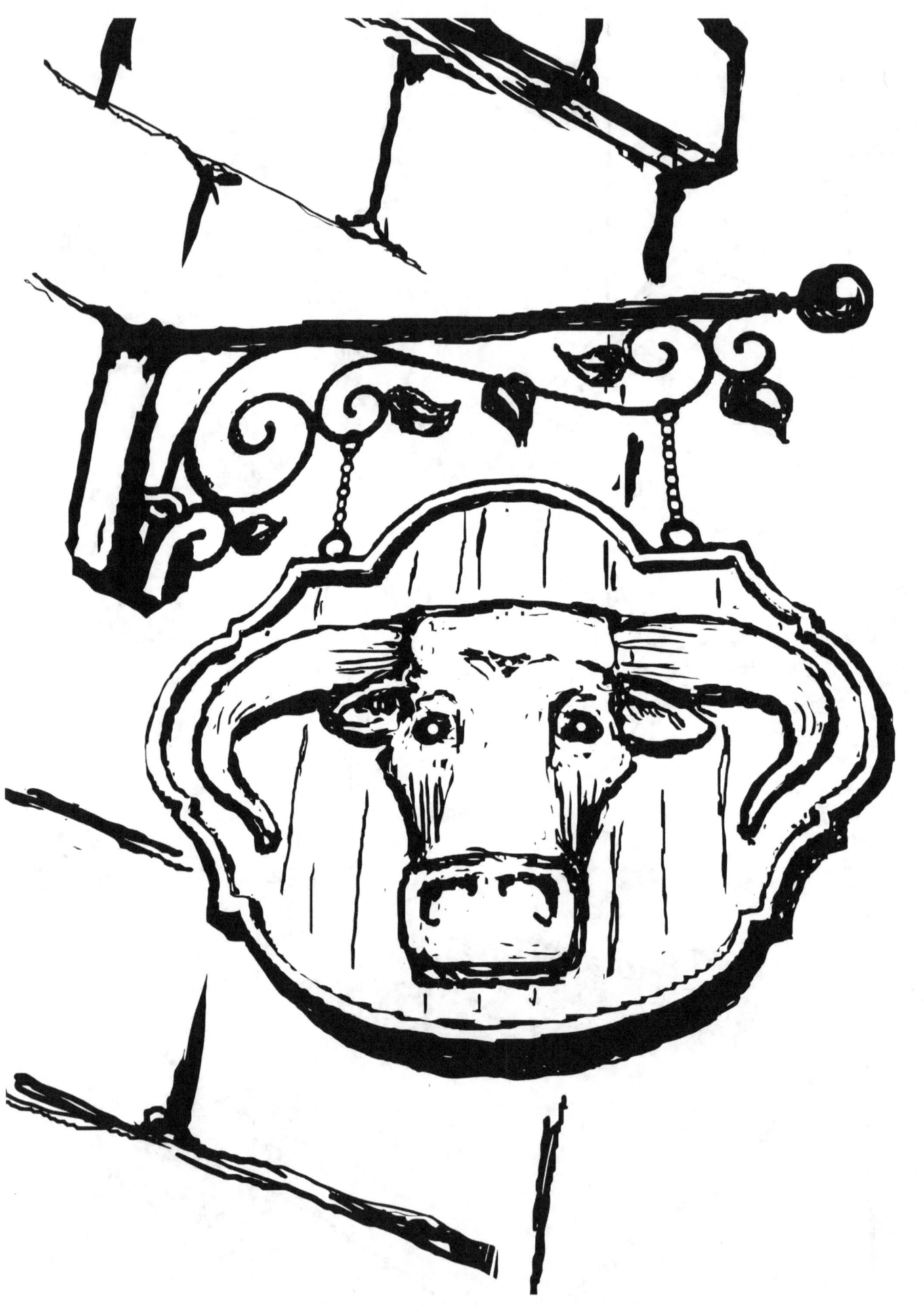

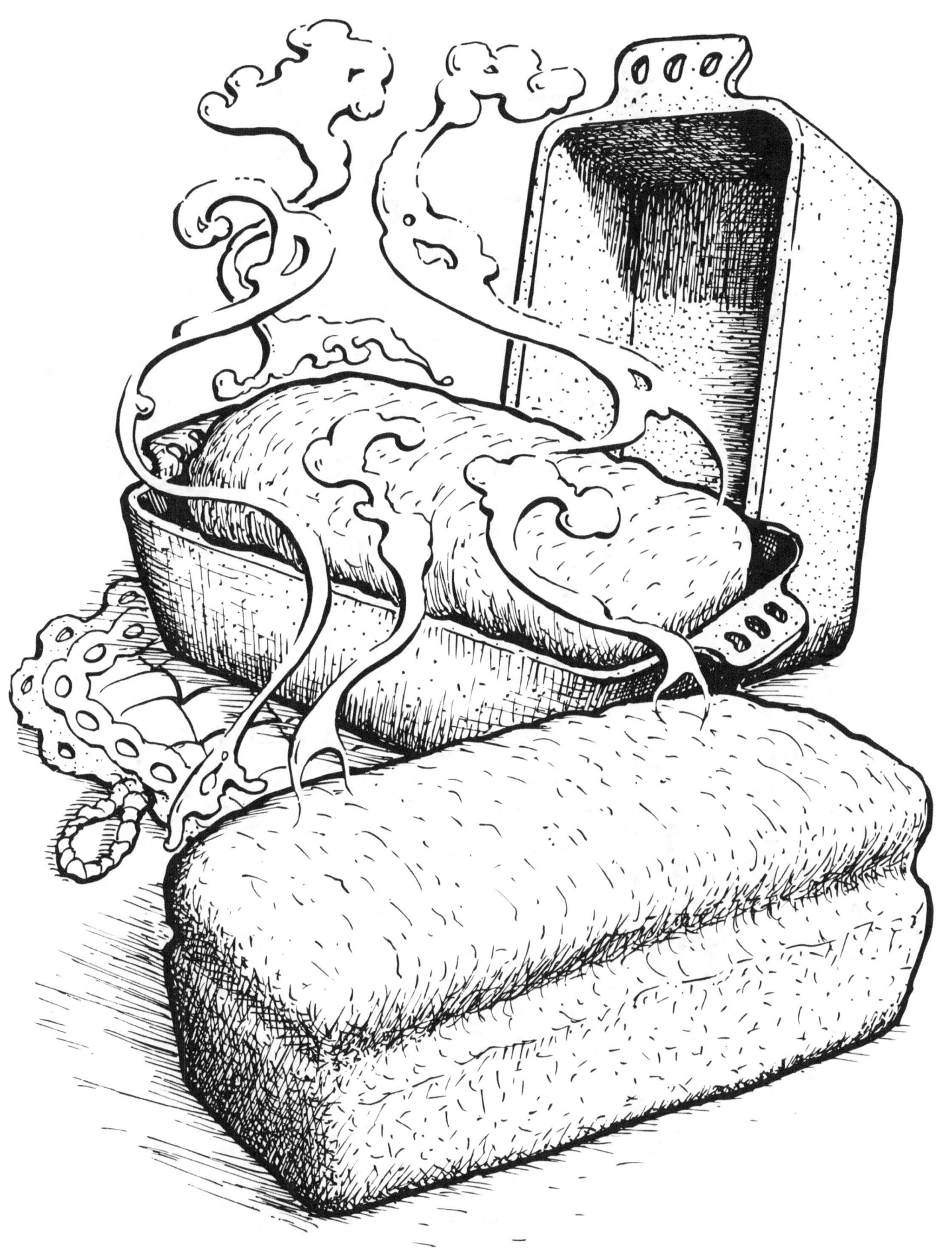